Watch Out, Ronald Morgan!

Also by Patricia Reilly Giff,
illustrated by Susanna Natti

Today Was a Terrible Day

The Almost Awful Play

Watch Out, Ronald Morgan!

by Patricia Reilly Giff

illustrated by Susanna Natti

Viking Kestrel

VIKING KESTREL

Viking Penguin Inc., 40 West 23rd Street, New York, New York 10010, U.S.A.
Penguin Books Ltd, Harmondsworth, Middlesex, England
Penguin Books Australia Ltd, Ringwood, Victoria, Australia
Penguin Books Canada Limited, 2801 John Street, Markham, Ontario, Canada L3R 1B4
Penguin Books (N.Z.) Ltd, 182–190 Wairau Road, Auckland 10, New Zealand

First published in 1985 by Viking Penguin Inc.
Published simultaneously in Canada

LIBRARY OF CONGRESS CATALOGING IN PUBLICATION DATA
Giff, Patricia Reilly.   Watch out, Ronald Morgan!
Summary: Ronald has many humorous mishaps until he gets a pair of eyeglasses.
Includes a note for adults about eye problems.
1. Children's stories, American. [1. Eyeglasses—Fiction] I. Natti, Susanna, ill.   II. Title.
PZ7.G3626Wat 1985   [E]   84-19623   ISBN 0-670-80433-9

Printed in Japan
by Dai Nippon
3 4 5 89 88 87
Set in Aster

*I would like to thank Dr. Frances Stavola, M.D., and Dr. David Shapiro, O.D., for their help with
this book.*
                                                                          P.R.G.

For my dear friend,
Carole Carnevale Hoffmann
P.R.G.

To Peter Eino
S.N.

It all started when the bell rang.
I raced across the school yard
and slid over a patch of ice.
"Watch out!" Rosemary yelled.
But it was too late.
I bumped into her
and she landed in a snow pile.

1

After I hung up my jacket,
I fed the goldfish.
I fed Frank, the gerbil, too.
"Oh, no," Rosemary said.
"You fed the gerbil food to Goldie."
"Oh," I said. "The boxes look the same."
Billy shook his head.

"Can't you read the letters?
F is for fish. G is for gerbil."
"Don't worry," said Michael, my best friend.
He poured more water into the fish tank.

At recess Miss Tyler wouldn't let us
go outside.
"You'll get snow in your sneakers,"
she said.
So we played kickball in the gym.
The ball bounced off my head.
Marc said, "I'm glad
you're not on my team."
And Rosemary said,
"Can't you even see the ball?"

Then it was time for book reports.

"Who'd like to be first?" Miss Tyler asked.

I ducked behind my desk.

"Ronald Morgan," said Miss Tyler.

"My book is *Lennie Lion*," I said.

I held up my report
and blinked to see the words.
"This book is about a lion
named Lennie.
He's ferocious and good."
"Great," said Jan.
"Grr," said Michael.
"Lovely," said Miss Tyler.

After lunch we looked out the window.
Everything was white.
"It's time for a winter classroom,"
said Miss Tyler.
I bent over my desk
and drew a snowflake.
Then I cut it out.
Tom said, "Ronald Morgan,
that's a wiggly snowflake.
Why don't you cut on the lines?"
And Rosemary said,
"I think your snowflake is melting."

When it was time to go home,
Miss Tyler gave me a note
for my mother and father.
"Maybe you need glasses," she said.

At lunch the next day, Marc asked,
"When do you get your glasses?"
I took a bite of my peanut butter sandwich.
"I go to the doctor today."
And Michael asked, "Can I go with you?"

In the shopping mall
we passed my father's tie store.
I waved to him
and he waved back.
In Doctor Sims's window
was a huge pair of eyeglasses.
Michael and I made believe
they belonged to a monster.

"Look at these Es," said Doctor Sims.

"Which way do they point?"

I squinted my eyes and pointed.

The Es looked smaller and smaller.

Then Doctor Sims said,

"It's hard for you to see them."

And my mother said,

"You'll look great in glasses."

"Yes," said the doctor.
"Glasses will help. They'll make
everything look sharp and clear."
Next we went to the counter.
I tried on a pair of red frames.
They slid down over my nose.

I tried round ones and square ones.
Then I put on blue frames
and looked in the mirror.
"Good," said my mother.
"Good," said Michael.
And Doctor Sims said,
"The lenses will be ready in an hour."

We went to the tie store.
"My glasses are great,"
I told my father.
He smiled.
"Now everything will look
the way it should," he said.

Then my glasses were ready.

"Just wait till tomorrow," I said.

"I'll be the best ballplayer,

the best reader,

the best speller,

the best everything."

"Wow," said Michael.

"Nice," said my mother.

"Yes," I told them.

"I'll be the superkid of the school.

Before school, I threw some snowballs.
"You missed!" Jimmy yelled,
and threw one at me.
It landed right on my nose.
Rosemary laughed.
"Your glasses need windshield wipers,"
she said.
But Michael looked worried.
"How come your glasses don't work?"

In the classroom, I hung up my jacket
and put my hat on the shelf.
"Where is our fish monitor?" asked Miss Tyler.
I ran to give Goldie some food.
This time I looked at the box.
The letters looked big and sharp.
"G is for Goldie," I said.
"F is for Frank."
"Oh, no," said Billy.
"F is for fish. G is for gerbil."
And Michael frowned.
"I don't think your glasses help."

I tiptoed into the closet
and put the glasses inside my hat.
Alice looked at me.
"Where are your blue glasses?" she whispered.
I shook my head.
"I have terrible glasses.
I'll never be the superkid
of the class."

When it was time to go home,
Miss Tyler gave me another note.
My mother helped me with some of the words.

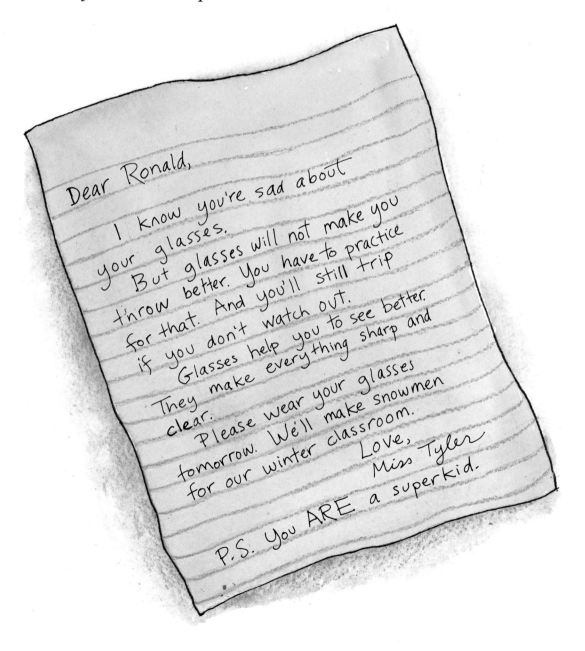

Dear Ronald,

I know you're sad about your glasses. But glasses will not make you throw better. You have to practice for that. And you'll still trip if you don't watch out. Glasses help you to see better. They make everything sharp and clear. Please wear your glasses tomorrow. We'll make snowmen for our winter classroom.

Love,
Miss Tyler

P.S. You ARE a superkid.

In school I drew a snowman
and picked up the scissors
to cut.
"Hey," I said,
"Miss Tyler's right.
The lines are sharp and clear."
"Good snowman," said Rosemary.

And Miss Tyler said,
"Just what we need for
our winter classroom."
I picked up my blue crayon
and drew a few more lines.
"Now he's a super snowman,"
I said.
We all cheered.

A Note for Parents and Teachers

Ronald Morgan has myopic astigmatism—distortion of objects seen at a distance. This means that, without glasses or contact lenses, sports will be extremely difficult for him, the blackboard will be blurry, and even the words in his reader will seem out of focus.

A child like Ronald, if his eyes are not checked and prescribed for, will learn to avoid ball playing. He may become a bookworm because that type of activity will be a little less uncomfortable for him—thus the stereotype. He will probably frown, squint, or blink. He may twist his head or his body to help him see more clearly. He'll bend over to make things come closer; eventually he may develop a serious problem with poor posture.

He may become withdrawn. Because he is unable to compete successfully in many popular sports and is hampered in certain classroom activities, he begins to believe he is not as "good", or as "smart" as his peers.

Children like Ronald may be tested by an ophthalmologist (a medical doctor who specializes in treatment and surgery of the eyes) or an optometrist (an expert in testing eyes for the prescription of glasses). An optician (a person trained in making and selling glasses) or an optometrist will fit the prescription lenses into frames that are comfortable. Then Ronald Morgan's vision will be as sharp as that of the rest of the children in Miss Tyler's class.   P.R.G.